A Midsummer Night's Dream

Sweet Cherry
Publishing

Published by Sweet Cherry Publishing Limited
Unit E, Vulcan Business Complex,
Vulcan Road,
Leicester, LE5 3EB,
United Kingdom

First published in the USA in 2013
ISBN: 978-1-78226-073-8

©Macaw Books

Title: A Midsummer Night's Dream
North American Edition

Text & Illustration by Macaw Books 2013

www.sweetcherrypublishing.com

Printed and bound by Wai Man Book Binding (China) Ltd. Kowloon, H.K.

~c◦ஃ About ஃ◦~
Shakespeare

William Shakespeare, regarded as the greatest writer in the English language, was born in Stratford-upon-Avon in Warwickshire, England (around April 23, 1564). He was the third of eight children born to John and Mary Shakespeare.

Shakespeare was a poet, playwright, and dramatist. He is often known as England's national poet and the "Bard of Avon." Thirty-eight plays, 154 sonnets, two long narrative poems, and several other poems are attributed to him. Shakespeare's plays have been translated into every major existent language and are performed more often than those of any other playwright.

Hermia: She is young, strong-willed, and independent. She does not hesitate to go against her father's wishes, even in the face of death. She is in love with a nobleman called Lysander. She is also loved by Demetrius, another nobleman, but she does not return his love.

Lysander: He is a young nobleman in Athens. He is in love with Hermia, though Hermia's father does not want his daughter to marry him. Lysander believes that he will be able to convince Hermia's father, so he persuades Hermia to run away with him.

Demetrius: Demetrius, another nobleman, is the favored son-in-law of Egeus, Hermia's father. Demetrius admitted once that he loved Hermia's friend, Helena, but later abandoned her. He pursues Hermia even though he knows she does not love him.

Oberon: Oberon is King of the Fairies. He wants to take revenge on his wife, Titania, Queen of the Fairies, and his method creates confusion and humor in the play.

A Midsummer Night's Dream

Once upon a time in Athens, there was a rather strict law regarding the marriage of girls. It had been decided by the Duke that every father had the right to give his daughter's hand in marriage to a man of his choice—and if his daughter were to refuse his offer, then she would be put to death. Now this

law was seldom carried out, as no father wanted to see his daughter dead, but in the case of Egeus and his daughter, Hermia, it was a different story altogether.

Egeus wanted Hermia to marry Demetrius, a noble youth to his liking. But Hermia knew that Demetrius had formerly professed his love for her dear friend Helena, who was madly in love with him. Of course, she did not mention that she herself was in love with a handsome man called Lysander, but she refused to obey her father's orders.

Theseus, the Duke of Athens, was a noble and kind ruler. He knew that Hermia's decision should be respected, but it was beyond his power to bend the law in her favor. So he gave her an ultimatum—she must either marry Demetrius in four days' time, or she would be sent to the gallows.

Hermia now faced a dilemma. She immediately went to Lysander and explained the problem to him. She told him that she only had four days to make up her mind, or she would die. Lysander said that one of his aunts lived not too far away, in a place where he knew this law

would not affect Hermia, as its
powers were limited to the city
of Athens. He asked her to run
away with him that night, and
told her he would wait for her
in the woods outside the city.

Hermia readily agreed
to this proposal and went off
to make preparations for the
escape. However, she made

one little mistake in the whole
plan. Like the innocent young
girl that she was, she told her
friend Helena about the plan,
who went and told Demetrius.
She knew that Demetrius would

surely follow Hermia to the woods that night, and she would follow him. Helena was in love with Demetrius, and to be in the woods at night with him was one of her oldest fantasies.

Little did everyone concerned know that the woods were the favorite haunt of tiny people known as fairies. Oberon was King of the Fairies and Titania was his queen. They would usually come out at midnight, along with their entourage of little fairies and elves.

However, during Hermia and Lysander's flight, the King and Queen of the Fairies were having a little disagreement. Their arguing had continued for several months, and whenever they started quarrelling, all the

little elves would run away
and hide out of fear.

The cause of the
disagreement was that one of
Titania's friends, upon her death,
had left the Queen of the Fairies

with a small child. Oberon now
wanted Titania to give him
that little boy as a page, an idea
Titania was completely averse to.

Now, on the night in
question, Titania was walking

through the woods with her maids-in-waiting, when suddenly Oberon and his merry band of men came before her. The minute Titania's eyes fell on her husband, she immediately asked her companions to leave. This infuriated Oberon, who said, "Am I not your lord, O rash fairy? Why do you cross me? Give me that little boy as my page."

But Titania merely turned her head away and replied, "Your entire fairy kingdom cannot buy the boy from me."

This brought greater anguish to
Oberon, who declared that before
dawn the next day, she would be
begging for his forgiveness. As
Titania left him, Oberon sent
for his favorite counselor, Puck.
   Puck was a clever and
naughty sprite who would while

away his time playing pranks
in the neighboring villages. He
would either spoil the milk, or,
using his magical powers, not
allow the cream to be churned
into butter. As if that were
not enough, he would make
people spill ale on themselves,

or would pull chairs out from under people seated on them.

Oberon asked the mischievous Puck to get him a purple flower called "Love in Idleness," the juice of which was a magic potion—when dropped on the eyelids of a person asleep, it would make them fall in love with the first person they saw upon waking up. Oberon knew of another magic potion that would make the charm created by this flower wear off, but he would not tell anyone about this until he had taken the little boy from Titania.

Puck, prankster that he was, was overjoyed at these

new orders and rushed off
immediately. While Oberon
waited for his partner in crime
to return, he saw Demetrius
walking into the forest, followed
by Helena. He could see
Demetrius trying to ward off

Helena, insulting her at every
opportunity, but the innocent
dame kept following him.

Oberon was always friendly
toward true lovers and felt
sorry for poor Helena. So when
Puck returned with the flower,

Oberon ordered
him to splash
some of the juice
on Demetrius's
eyelids if he could
catch him asleep. All
that Puck needed to remember
was to make sure that when
Demetrius awoke, it was Helena
he saw first. As Puck left to carry
out his assignment, Oberon
walked off to find Titania.

The Queen of the Fairies
was about to fall asleep, while
the fairies were busy singing
her a lullaby. Within a few
moments, Titania was fast
asleep. Oberon walked up to
her and dropped the liquid

onto her eyelids, saying, "What you see when you wake, do it for your true love take."

While Oberon was trying to convince Titania to hand over the little boy to him through magic, Hermia and Lysander arrived in the woods. When they were a short distance from Athens, Hermia declared that she was very tired and wanted to rest for the night. So the two

lovers lay down on a bed of moss and were soon fast asleep. Just then, Puck turned up

and concluded that these must be the two people his king had told him about. Without more ado, he poured the juice of the wondrous purple flower onto Lysander's eyelids and left. So, when Lysander next opened his eyes, the first person he would see was Helena, not Hermia.

Now, it so happened that Demetrius, tired of being followed around by Helena, had started to run and was soon out of her sight. Walking sadly through the woods, Helena had come upon the sleeping pair, Hermia and Lysander. Overjoyed at finding them, she nudged Lysander to wake him up. And the magic began…

The minute he saw Helena, Lysander began expressing his love for her. Helena was naturally shocked to hear him speak that way. She knew that he was madly in

love with Hermia and thought
he was making fun of her. This
made her very upset. Telling him
that she had not expected this,
Helena ran away, tears streaming
down her face, while a distraught
Lysander was left wondering
what had happened. He had

obviously forgotten all about Hermia, who was still fast asleep.

By the time Hermia awoke, Lysander was gone. Meanwhile, Demetrius, who was searching the forest for Hermia and Lysander, realized he was lost.

Since he was very tired now, he decided to stop for a while and rest. He soon fell asleep.

Oberon, who was passing through the forest at that time, saw Demetrius asleep. Puck had told him about the blunder and, finding

the original recipient of his
scheme, decided to act himself.
He poured a few drops of the
magical juice onto Demetrius's
eyelids and left him to sleep.

When Demetrius woke up,
lo and behold! The first person
he saw was Helena. As he started
to give the same speech that

Lysander had made to her before, Lysander arrived in search of Helena. Then they both started to woo the mystified Helena.

Hermia, who was searching the woods for her beloved Lysander, arrived and could not believe what she was seeing. Helena was now of the impression that all three of them had decided to make fun of her and she was seething. Soon the two women got into a war of words, and the men decided to find a suitable place where they could fight over Helena.

Oberon was completely taken aback by recent developments.

He was furious with Puck
for having messed up earlier.
Puck replied that it was
hardly his fault—Oberon had
merely asked him to find two
lovers, which he had done.

Oberon realized that since he had caused this mess, it was up to him to resolve it. He ordered Puck to create a thick fog over the woods immediately, which would result in all four

friends losing each other. He also told Puck to lead the two men away, so that they became so tired they would be unable to walk any further. Then he gave him some juice from another plant, which would cause the effects of the purple flower to wear off. Puck was told to drop this liquid onto Lysander's eyelids, so that when he awoke he would forget all about Helena and go back to Hermia.

Oberon left in search
of Titania. He found her still
asleep and so dropped the
magic potion onto her eyelids.
Nearby, he found a clown
asleep as well. Through his
magic, he replaced the clown's
head with that of a donkey and
woke him up. As the foolish

clown wandered along,
he came across Titania, who
was beginning to rouse. When
she saw the joker with the
donkey's head, she immediately
fell in love with him.
Oberon's trick was working!

Titania immediately asked
her maids to tend to the man
who had completely taken over
her heart. The clown, who had
no idea about the donkey's
head on his shoulders, was

overjoyed at the services he was being offered and decided to sleep again in comfort.

As Titania held his head in her arms and crowned it with flowers, Oberon made his appearance. He bellowed at her, accusing her of taking a donkey for a lover and being unfaithful to him. Titania was ashamed of herself, but there was little she could do. The magic had done its work.

Oberon, playing on Titania's guilt, once again asked for the boy. Obviously, the Queen of the Fairies was in no position to fight with her husband now that she had been caught stroking a donkey

in her arms. So, without wasting
any more time, she immediately
sent for the boy and handed him
over to Oberon as his page.

Now that Oberon had got
what he wanted, he immediately
reversed the magic potion with

 the help of the
other juice and
gave the clown
his head back.
Titania came to
her senses and
Oberon told her
what he had done. Although
Titania was angry initially, she
soon relented, and the king
and queen were reconciled.

Oberon then told his
beloved wife about the lovers.
Titania was intrigued and they
set off to find the confused
mortals. The royal fairies
saw that Puck had managed
to bring all four friends to
the same spot without them

knowing. Since they were now
asleep, Puck dropped the new
liquid that Oberon had given
him onto Lysander's eyelids.

Hermia was the first to
wake up. She found Lysander
sleeping next to her, and as

she was wondering why he
had suddenly started acting so
strangely, he opened his eyes and
saw her. He had now forgotten
all about his love for Helena,
and he stared into Hermia's eyes
like he had done so many times
before. Hermia told him what

had happened to them, but Lysander could not remember anything. They left together, thinking that it all must have been a dream.

Helena and Demetrius also woke up shortly after. Helena was much calmer after her restful sleep, while Demetrius continued in the same tone as before. Helena thought he must be speaking the truth and was very happy with the way things had turned out.

When Helena and Hermia met again later that day, they reconciled their differences and

were once again the best
of friends. They talked
about everything that had
happened the night before, but

decided to forget about it as they
had all got what they wanted.

Demetrius, now in love with
Helena, no longer wanted to
marry Hermia, so it was decided

that they would all go back to
Athens, where Demetrius would
inform Egeus of his decision.
They hoped that would persuade
Hermia's father to repeal the
death sentence against her.

Just as they were setting off
for Athens, Egeus arrived. He
had discovered his daughter
had run away and had come to
the woods in search of her.

Demetrius told Egeus that he no longer wished to marry his daughter, so Egeus could now allow Hermia to marry Lysander. Egeus declared that they would get married on the fourth day, the day on which Hermia would have been put to death. Demetrius and Helena also decided to marry on that day.

Oberon and Titania witnessed these events and were overjoyed. Oberon immediately announced a night of revelry throughout the fairy kingdom.